Edited by Anna McQuinn and Ambreen Husain
Designed by Suzy McGrath and Sarah Godwin

First published in the United States in 1996 by
De Agostini Editions Ltd, 919 Third Avenue,
New York, NY 10022

Distributed by Stewart, Tabori & Chang
a division of U.S. Media Holdings, Inc.,
New York, NY

ISBN 1-899883-62-2
Library of Congress Catalog Card Number:
96-84149

Printed and bound in Italy

Food Science Consultant
Shirley Corriher

For Alice, CF

My Grandma is GREAT!

Written by

Hannah Roche

Illustrated by

Chris Fisher

DeA

My grandma is great!

Today she mixed some sugar and butter
in a bowl – first it was grainy, but she
kept beating until it was nice and smooth.

I mixed some flour, baking soda, salt and
spices in another bowl – it was lots of fun!

Next Grandma mixed together some molasses and water. Then, little by little, she added this and the flour to the buttery mix.

When it got really stretchy,
Grandma made it into a ball
and put it in the fridge. She said
that would make it less sticky.

After an hour, she took it out again.
She sprinkled flour all over the table
and put the fat ball of dough on top.

We got a rolling pin and we rolled and rolled.
The fat ball of dough got flatter and flatter,
thinner and thinner,
and wider and wider.

My grandma is great!

Then I got my cookie cutter and cut
lots of little circles out of the dough.

Next I made two little men
and Grandma made a little woman.

Then we made three dogs and a cow!

We put on some raisins for the eyes,
and cherries for the mouths.

Then Grandma put them in the oven.
"Don't touch the oven," she said,
"it's hot!"

Abracadabra!
They had turned into **cookies!**
You should let them cool down
but I sneaked one while
they were still warm.

It was yummy
and crispy
and a little
bit crumbly!

I love my grandma.
She's great!

Yum!

Notes for Parents

EVEN very young children are aware that water is wet, rock is hard, sand is grainy. As they observe more, children discover that things don't always stay the same – rolling, heating, mixing, freezing and so on make things change from soft to hard, from round to flat, from liquid to solid....

LEARNING to notice and describe the textures and changes is important to children's understanding of the world around them. Don't worry about using "proper" scientific words – getting the description right is what really matters.

YOU can recreate the story in your own kitchen by following the recipe opposite. As you go along, encourage your child to talk about what's happening. Then, you can eat the results!

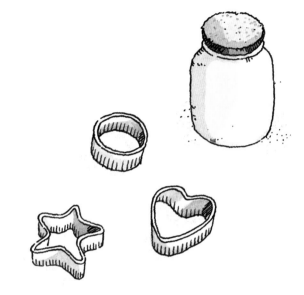

HOW IT WORKS

AS YOU mix the ingredients to make the dough, the butter gets softer and melts. If you rolled out the dough at this stage, it would be too soft and sticky.

PUTTING the dough in the fridge will make it stiff again. It's tricky to get it just right – if it's too cold it will crack around the edges, so you may have to let it sit for a few minutes before you roll it out.

Millie's Recipe

YOU WILL NEED:

2½ cups of all-purpose flour

½ teaspoon of baking soda

½ teaspoon of salt

1 level teaspoon of ground ginger

¼ teaspoon of ground nutmeg

⅛ teaspoon of ground allspice

½ cup of butter

½ cup of sugar

¼ cup of water

½ cup of dark molasses

raisins for the eyes

cherries for the mouths

bowls, a whisk or electric mixer, a rolling pin, cookie cutters, wax paper or plastic, a baking sheet, spoons for mixing, teaspoons and a wire rack

HINTS

MAKING the dough into a ball and then pressing it into a disc before refrigerating makes it easier to roll out.

1. Stir together the flour, baking soda, salt and spices. Mix well.

2. In a large bowl, beat together the butter and sugar until light and creamy.

3. Mix the water and molasses and gradually add this and the flour mixture to the butter and sugar.

4. Beat together until all the ingredients are combined, but do not overmix.

5. Gather the dough into a ball, press it into a disc, wrap it in wax paper or plastic and chill in the refrigerator for at least an hour.

6. Preheat your oven to 375°F/180°C.

7. Place the chilled dough on a lightly floured table top, sprinkle some flour on top, then roll it out to about ⅛" thick.

8. Cut the dough into shapes and place on the baking sheet, at least ½" apart.

9. Bake for 8–12 minutes or until they turn golden around the edges. Then remove from the oven and let cool for a few minutes before transferring to a wire rack.

DATE DUE